Famou Lanum...

Ryder Shava

Rosen
REAL
READERS

Rosen
Classroom™
New York

There are many famous **landmarks** in America. This is the Capitol Building. It is where laws are passed.

The White House is where the President lives. Every president has lived here since 1801. This is where Presidents do most of their work. The Capitol Building and the White House are in Washington, D.C.

The Washington **monument** was built to honor George Washington. The monument is over 500 feet tall!

IN THIS TEMPLE
AS IN THE HEARTS OF THE PEOPLE
FOR WHOM HE SAVED THE UNION
THE MEMORY OF ABRAHAM LINCOLN
IS ENSHRINED FOREVER

The Lincoln Memorial was built to honor Abraham Lincoln. There is a large **statue** of Lincoln inside the memorial. The Washington Monument and the Lincoln Memorial are in Washington, D.C.

The Smithsonian Institution is also in Washington, D.C. It was built In 1846. It includes museums, research centers, and a zoo.

The Golden Gate Bridge is one of the most famous bridges in America. It is located in San Francisco, California. It is one of the Seven Wonders of the Modern World.

Mount Rushmore is in South Dakota. It is
a memorial to four U.S. Presidents. Their
faces are carved into a mountain. It took
14 years to make.

The Statue of Liberty is in New York Harbor. It was given to America by France in 1886. It was made in France, and then put together in America.

This is Independence Hall. It is in Philadelphia. This is where the Declaration of Independence was signed. The U.S. Constitution was signed here, too.

The Hoover **Dam** is on the Colorado River. It is between Nevada and Arizona. The dam was named after Herbert Hoover. Hoover was the 31st President of the United States.

Glossary

dam   A wall that is built across a river or stream to stop water from flowing.

landmarks   Well-known objects, buildings, or structures.

monument   A building, structure, or statue that honors a person or event.

statue   A figure made from stone or metal.